The Adventures of Milo & Otis

by Mark Saltzman

SCHOLASTIC INC.
New York Toronto London Auckland Sydney

Creative services by Parachute Press, Inc.

Designed by Greg Wozney Design

ISBN 0-590-42691-5

12 11 10 9 8 7 6 5 4 3 2 1   9/8 0 1 2 3 4/9

Printed in the U.S.A.   34

First Scholastic printing, April 1989

Except for the activity up in the hayloft, the farm was pretty quiet that morning.

Inside the barn the farm dogs slept on their backs, their paws curled in the air. The noise upstairs didn't disturb them. They could sleep through anything!

But a lot of the other animals were awakened by all that scratching and squealing and scurrying overhead. Some went right back to sleep. But the ducks in the corner were very annoyed. And the rabbits were talking about ways to get even.

Up in the hayloft, the mood was very different. The farm cat had been awake all night giving birth to kittens. And now the tiny kittens were crying for their breakfast.

One of the kittens—the one named Milo—was trouble from the very beginning.

Like his brothers and sisters, Milo was ginger colored with soft, white fur on his stomach and paws. But there was a mischievous sparkle in Milo's wide dark eyes. While the other kittens climbed over each other to get their breakfast, Milo decided to go exploring.

"Milo, come back here!" his mother cried.

She caught him in her teeth and gently carried him back to the others.

"Don't go looking for trouble, Milo," she scolded. "Trouble will find you soon enough!"

A few weeks later Milo met Otis, one of the barn puppies.

Otis was a stout little pug, with a pushed-in pug face, floppy pug ears, and a curly pug tail that never stopped wagging.

It didn't take long for Milo and Otis to become best friends.

They rolled and wrestled in the soft barn hay. They nipped and yipped, chasing each other from one side of the barn to the other, squealing and biting and tumbling about.

They even napped together, snuggling all cozy and warm in a fragrant bed of hay.

What fun!

A few weeks later, Milo's mother took the kittens outside to show them the world beyond the hayloft. There were so many exciting things to see on the big farm.

"Milo, get away from that hen!" his mother cried. "I've told you again and again—don't walk on the chickens!"

Then one morning, Milo's mother took the kittens to the river. The kittens stared down at the sparkling blue waters.

"When you're on the dock, don't go too close to the edge," their mother warned.

"What's too close? Is this?" Milo asked, stepping to the edge of the dock. All at once his front paw slipped and he fell into the river with a splash. The water carried the frightened kitten downstream.

Milo's mother jumped into the water and began swimming after him as fast as she could. The current carried Milo to a log in the middle of the river. He eagerly climbed onto it, and soon his mother climbed on too.

"Are you all right?" she asked, licking him all over.

"Yes," Milo whimpered quietly.

"That's good, Milo. Because you're in deep trouble!" his mother said.

But trouble certainly wasn't anything new to Milo!

The next day, the henhouse was in an uproar. The cackling and clucking could be heard all over the farm. Milo and Otis went to see what the fuss was about.

"Okay, clear out!" a chicken named Gloria shouted. Gloria was terribly excited because she had just laid her first egg.

"Keep an eye on it, Otis," she said proudly, "while I go out and tell everyone on the farm about it!"

Gloria ran off and Milo and Otis were left with the shiny new egg. "Hey, Otis," Milo said playfully, "do you think eggs bounce?"

"Cut that out!" Otis barked. "Gloria gave us a job to do."

Otis took the job very seriously. He put his nose right up to the egg so he could watch it closely. And when he and Milo took a nap, they slept with the egg nestled between them.

"This is a big day for me," Otis said. "This is the day I have become a watchdog!"

"How long do we have to stick around this henhouse?" Milo asked. He was bored. So when he heard some strange noises in the trees, Milo went out to investigate.

The noises were being made by a baby bird who was trying to sing. "Stop it! You can't sing! Stop it!" Milo begged.

But the stubborn bird kept screeching.

"What's all the noise? I'm trying to watch an egg!" Otis barked, running out of the henhouse.

While Milo and Otis were outside, they thought the egg would be safe. But they were wrong. A hungry hedgehog sneaked into the henhouse. "Here's my lunch!" he said.

Milo and Otis came running to the rescue. "Freeze!" Otis growled. "Don't touch that egg!"

He barked and growled ferociously until the hedgehog backed away. "Okay, okay," the frightened hedgehog said. "Who wants your egg anyway? It's probably rotten." And the hedgehog waddled off.

Milo's attention was on the egg, which was starting to wobble and shake.

"Otis, look," Milo said, staring at the egg. "I think we're having a baby!"

Milo and Otis watched as a baby chick, all wet and sticky, pushed its way out of the egg. A few moments later the little yellow chick struggled to its feet and cheeped hello.

Milo and Otis were very proud and happy. Ducks and rabbits and other farm animals crowded into the henhouse to get a look at the baby chick.

They brought the chick to Gloria, but it kept coming back to Otis. "Mommy," said the chick to the surprised dog.

They tried to make the mixed-up chick join the other chickens. But the little creature hopped right back to Otis.

Then Otis got an idea. "Okay, you want to be a dog?" he said to the chick. "Here's what you have to do. You've got to be a rough, tough, fighting dog like me!" And with that, Otis jumped on Milo and began wrestling with him.

"Mommy! Chicken Mommy!" the chick cried. And he ran to Gloria.

Otis let go of Milo. "Thanks for helping out," he told his friend. "I'll miss the little guy. But at least he figured out that he's a chicken!"

One sunny afternoon Otis and Milo went down to the dock by the river. Otis wanted to stretch out and sun himself. But Milo wanted to play.

The lively cat saw a wooden box floating in the water. He leaped off the dock and into the box, to hide from Otis.

"Hey, Milo!" Otis cried, greatly alarmed. "Get out of that box before something happens!"

Too late!

The river currents began to carry the box downstream. "Oh, no!" Otis cried, watching helplessly from the dock as the box carrying Milo floated farther and farther away.

Otis began to run along the shore, trying to keep up with Milo. But the grass was tall and wet, and Otis's little legs kept slipping out from under him.

Milo looked back at his friend as the box began to float downstream faster and faster. "I'm coming, Milo!" Otis cried. He jumped into the water and began swimming toward his friend, his little paws splashing furiously.

Otis swam as fast as he could, trying to catch up. But the river was flowing too fast. Soon Otis couldn't see Milo or the box anywhere.

Milo wasn't worried until he lost sight of Otis. But when he realized his friend was far behind, Milo felt scared and terribly alone.

Suddenly he heard something moving in the thick bushes along the bank of the river. Was it Otis? Milo peeked over the side of the box.

No. It definitely was not Otis. It was a big brown bear, searching along the riverbank for food. Milo ducked down low, hoping the bear hadn't seen him. But the box was drifting right toward the big, hungry bear.

Poor Milo's eyes opened wide with fright as the bear waded into the water and grabbed the box. Growling hungrily, the bear reached out a big paw to grab Milo.

Suddenly Otis appeared on the shore. He saw at once what was happening. "Oh, no you don't!" he cried, and he leaped into the water and swam over to fight the bear.

The bear turned in surprise. Did this little dog really think he could win a fight against a full-grown bear?

Otis began wrestling in the water with the startled bear. He put up a good fight. But the bear was too powerful for him.

Suddenly Otis had a better idea. He began to swim away. His plan was to lead the bear out of the water and away from Milo.

Otis swam to shore. The bear was right behind him. His plan had worked! Now the bear was chasing him and had forgotten all about Milo.

Otis ran fast. After a while, he looked behind him and the bear was gone.

Milo was worried. The river was flowing faster and faster. He was being tossed back and forth as the box rushed over sharp, jutting rocks.

Milo peeked over the top of the box and what he saw filled him with terror. He shut his eyes tight. The box was headed for a steep, steep waterfall! "I'm not going to make it!" he told himself. "I'm not going to make it!"

Water splashed over the top of the box. Milo was being bounced harder and harder. Would his box break apart on the rocks? Would Milo be tossed into the rushing waters? It was the scariest moment of Milo's life.

Down, down he fell.

When he opened his eyes, Milo saw that he had landed safely. Except for being scared and wet, Milo was okay. The river had slowed, carrying him more gently now. He looked back, hoping to see Otis. But his friend was nowhere in sight.

Otis was far behind. He had outrun the bear and he was still determined to rescue his friend. He ran along the shore, keeping his eyes on the river, hoping to see Milo.

Soon the brave little dog came to a scary place, a place like none he'd ever seen before. It was the Deadwood Swamp.

Otis stopped and looked around. The ground was soft and wet, with deep pools of muddy water. Bare and broken trees grew without leaves or branches. No creatures could live in such a bare and ugly place—except for the black, long-beaked ravens called the Deadwood Birds.

There, a few feet in front of him, a Deadwood Bird stood perched on a familiar wooden box. It was Milo's box!

Was Milo safe and sound inside the box? Otis had to find out.

He ran over the sticky ground up to the ugly Deadwood Bird.

Otis's heart was pounding. He took a deep breath and looked into the box. Milo?

But inside was . . . only a single black feather.

Milo was far away from the Deadwood Swamp. After his box got stuck in the bog, he had run away from the Deadwood Birds.

He ran until he came to a meadow of tall grass. Now he was tired and hungry. He hadn't eaten for an entire day.

Suddenly he saw something moving quickly through the tall grass. It was a fox. "Foxes always have some goodies stashed away," Milo told himself. Keeping out of sight, he began to follow the fox.

The fox ran quickly, sniffing the air nervously as if he suspected he was being followed. When he came to a sandy beach, he stopped and dug up a treat he had buried there—a tasty muskrat.

Milo watched from a low tree limb as the fox moved his prize to a safer hiding place. Then, when the fox ran off, Milo climbed down and dug up the muskrat.

Yum! What a delicious lunch!

Otis's search for Milo brought him to a wide beach, where he climbed on a rock to look around. Suddenly the clouds grew darker and a cold wind began to blow. Then the tide came in so fast that the rock Otis was standing on was completely surrounded by deep water. "What shall I do?" Otis asked himself. "Soon the rock will be underwater. The beach is so far away. I'll never be able to swim to shore."

When the water was up to his paws, Otis had no choice. He had to try to swim. He took a deep breath and prepared to dive into the swirling water.

But just then he heard a deep voice in the water beside him saying, "Not again!"

A large sea turtle floated up to Otis's rock. "Every time the tide comes in, some fool gets stuck out here," the turtle grumbled.

Otis wasn't sure what this grumpy creature wanted.

"Look—do you want a ride back to shore or don't you?" the turtle asked.

Otis didn't have to be asked twice. He climbed onto the turtle's broad shell. Slowly, carefully, the big turtle swam to shore with Otis clinging tightly to him.

"Just stay on land where you belong," the turtle muttered, and turned back into the water.

"Don't worry. I will!" Otis called after him happily. "And thanks for saving me." And then he ran across the beach to continue his search for Milo.

The sky turned sunny and bright. The air felt crisp and fresh. Otis ran from the beach and arrived at a riverbank.

Suddenly he heard some loud singing. He looked in the water and saw the fox, splashing about in the waves, having a wonderful bath and singing at the top of his lungs.

"Maybe that fox can be helpful," Otis told himself. He waited for the fox to finish his swim and his song, and then he ran up to him.

"Have you seen an orange cat?" he asked.

"Maybe I did and maybe I didn't," the fox said snootily. And then he remembered. "Wait a minute! You know, there was a nasty, hole-digging, lunch-stealing cat here just a short while ago! He stole my muskrat."

"Yes! Yes! That sounds like him!" cried Otis happily. "Thank you! Thanks a lot!"

The confused fox stared at Otis. "What are you so happy about?"

But Otis had already run off, very excited to learn that he was getting closer to finding his friend.

What a long journey. Poor Milo was worn out. He decided to rest for a while, and settled down in a place that looked comfortable and safe. But he had made a terrible mistake.

Milo was resting in the middle of a railroad track!

He had almost fallen asleep when a loud roar made him look up. A train was coming toward him at full speed.

Milo froze in fright. He didn't know what to do. He couldn't move. The train came closer . . . closer . . .

Milo ducked.

And the train went right over him.

Whew! He was safe.

But he knew he had to find a better place to sleep!

After his close call, Milo ran until he came to a beautiful meadow full of yellow flowers. "Now I'm really tired," he told himself. "If only someone could help me find a snug place to rest."

"You look tired and thirsty, friend," a voice said.

Milo looked up to see a young doe. Her big brown eyes stared down at him tenderly. "Follow me," she said softly.

The doe leaped over the flowers. Milo could barely keep up with her. Across the meadow she darted and jumped, with Milo stumbling behind.

She led him to a thick, leafy glade. There they found a safe, cozy spot between the trees and lay down in the soft, sweet-smelling grass.

The doe nuzzled Milo tenderly. They snuggled close together. Soon they fell into a lovely, peaceful nap.

When Milo woke from his sleep, he left the deer in her glade and began traveling deep into a forest. Now there were different noises and new creatures to worry about. And night was coming soon.

Milo climbed a tree and decided to stay up there until daylight. There was even an empty nest on the branch and Milo snuggled into it.

Suddenly, a snowy white owl swooped down and snatched up a field mouse in its sharp talons. Then the owl flew back up to its branch to enjoy its meal.

"Wow!" thought Milo, "Look how easily he scooped up that poor mouse. I'd better stay out of sight."

Just then he heard a frightened squeal. "Help. Please. Some body help me!" Who could that be?

"Help me! Please help me!" the little voice squealed again.

Milo found a pink baby pig with his foot caught in a bramble. "Hurry!" the frightened pig cried. "That owl will be back!"

"Take it easy, little fella," Milo said. He worked quickly and untangled the pig's foot. "You're fine now. Do you know a place where we'll be safe?"

"Yes. With my family," squealed the pig. "Come with me."

Milo followed the little pig through the forest until they came to his family. And what a family! The little pig had at least ten brothers and sisters!

They all squealed with joy when they saw their little brother return. Then they welcomed Milo warmly and gave him a place to sleep—cuddled up with them!

The next morning Milo woke up and thought, "These pigs are all right—friendly and kind. Just a nice bunch of pigs."

But then the mother pig squealed, "BREAKFAST! COME AND GET IT!" The little pigs pushed and shoved and climbed over each other to get to their meal. Their table manners came as quite a shock to Milo.

"Good heavens!" he thought. "No wonder they call them pigs!"

After breakfast, Milo said goodbye to his friends and traveled through the woods until at the end of the day he found himself at a gentle green brook. Peering into the clear water, he could see some delicious-looking trout.

"I'm so hungry," Milo thought. "How can I catch a nice trout for my dinner?"

He thought and thought and finally came up with an idea. He turned his back to the brook and dangled his tail in the water. "My tail makes a perfect fishing line," he told himself. He stood as still as he could, hoping for a trout to grab his tail.

Milo didn't know that a raccoon was watching from a tree limb above the brook. "That silly cat has got to be kidding!" the raccoon muttered.

Then a big, juicy trout grabbed Milo's tail, and he pulled it out of the water. "I've caught one!" Milo cried.

"You've caught one for me!" the raccoon said. He leaped down from the tree limb and grabbed Milo's fish. "Nice fish," the raccoon said with a sneer. "Too bad it's gonna be the one that got away!"

"Come back with my fish!" Milo cried.

The raccoon just laughed and ran off with it. But the raccoon wasn't the only one interested in Milo's fish.

Suddenly the brown bear jumped out from behind a tree and grabbed the trout out of the raccoon's paws.

The raccoon grabbed it back.

The bear took a swipe at the raccoon with its huge, brown paw. The raccoon ducked. The bear made another grab for the fish, but the raccoon stubbornly hung on.

It was a terrible fight.

Milo climbed a tree to watch.

The bear and the raccoon battled over the trout until the bear saw something bigger and tastier—

MILO!

A few seconds later, the bear was on the same branch as Milo. He began inching himself closer, closer to the frightened cat.

Milo was trapped. He had no choice but to fight. He swung his paw at the bear's nose.

The bear backed away. He didn't like that.

The brave cat swung at the bear again and again until the bear lost his footing and fell to the forest floor with a loud crash.

Milo was safe but when he looked around, the raccoon had disappeared with his trout. So Milo, still hungry, traveled on.

Meanwhile, Otis kept up his long search for his friend. He had trailed Milo from Deadwood Swamp to the fox's river. He knew he was on the right track. He was certain that if he just kept going, he'd find Milo. He tried to keep up his spirits. But it was hard. He missed Milo so much!

Soon Milo came to the top of a high rock cliff. He saw some seagulls and knew that seagull nests were a likely place to find some tasty eggs.

Suddenly from up above a seagull screamed, "Cat! A cat! There's a cat near the babies!"

"A cat! A cat!" squawked a chorus of seagulls. "Get him!"

Several of the big white birds swooped down on Milo. They flapped their wings in his face and pecked at his shoulders and head.

Milo had no choice. He had to get away the fastest way possible. So he dived off the high cliff into the water below.

A few minutes later, Milo climbed out of the sea, feeling wet, sticky, and cold. And he looked a lot more like a wet mop than a cat!

Milo climbed onto the beach and looked for a place where he could dry off. Up ahead he saw a small wooden shack. He crept up to it and peeked through the broken front door. There was no one inside.

"It looks warm and safe in there," he told himself. "I think I'll stay here for a while until I dry off and get some rest."

He went inside, shook himself to get some of the water off, then found a cozy spot in a corner where he could take a long nap and forget about those horrible seagulls.

He was just about asleep when a noise outside startled him. Milo ran to the shack window and looked out.

There, frolicking in the water just a few yards from the shack, was the brown bear!

"Stay calm," Milo told himself, watching the bear splash and play in the water. "I'll be all right as long as he doesn't come—UH-OH!"

Milo couldn't stay calm any longer because the bear had climbed out of the water and was walking right toward the shack. "Where can I hide? Where can I go?" Milo asked himself, frantically looking around the tiny room.

The brown bear knew that someone was in the shack. He pulled open the door and burst in.

Milo dived into a drawer of a battered old dresser. The bear growled and began searching for him.

"Please don't find me. Please don't find me," Milo repeated.

But the bear spotted Milo's tail sticking out of the dresser drawer. He hurried over and grabbed it in his teeth.

"Let go of me!" Milo cried. "Let go!"

Milo leaped out of the dresser drawer onto a high shelf.

"Where'd you go? Where'd you go?" cried the angry bear. The bear couldn't find Milo. He searched all around. Then he decided that Milo must have run outside, so he turned and ran down the beach looking for him.

Milo crept out from his hiding place on the shelf. "That bear will be back," he told himself. "I think I'll be a lot safer hiding in the top of a tall tree."

But he was wrong again.

No sooner had Milo reached a low branch than a long, silvery snake came slithering up after him.

Milo quickly climbed to a higher branch. But the snake climbed higher, too, hissing at him.

Milo realized he had to fight again. He hissed back at the snake and swiped at it with his paw.

But before the snake could attack, Milo's branch snapped.

Down Milo fell. Down, down, into a deep hole in the ground.

Milo tried to jump out of the hole. But it was too deep. He tried to climb out. But the sides were too steep.

He was trapped.

He started calling for help, even though he knew it was useless. Nobody could hear him out there.

But somebody did. Milo couldn't believe his eyes when Otis's familiar face peeked down from the top of the hole. "Otis—is it really you?" he cried.

Otis was happy too. He had finally found his friend. "Don't worry," Otis barked. "I'll get you out . . . somehow."

And then he disappeared. A short while later Otis returned with a rope he had found. He tossed one end down to Milo. "Grab on to it. I'll pull you out," he said.

Milo grabbed one end with his teeth and paws. Otis clenched his teeth hard on the other end of the rope. Then he pulled and pulled.

"We did it! We did it!" Otis cried, opening his mouth by mistake.

Poor Milo fell back into the hole.

They tried again. This time Otis kept his teeth tightly clenched until Milo was safely on the ground.

Then what a happy time they had! They ran and leaped and wrestled. They were bursting with joy because they were finally back together.

Starting for home, Otis and Milo heard a cat crying in the distance. They ran to investigate.

Milo's eyes grew wide when he first saw her. She was a beautiful female, as white as snow. "Hello," she purred. "My name is Joyce."

Milo was breathless. For him, it was love at first sight.

As the days went by, Milo and Joyce became friendlier and friendlier. Milo was spending all of his time with Joyce and ignoring Otis.

"Joyce," Milo said softly. "Come back with me to my farm. Everyone will love you. I love you."

Joyce said yes. She led the way out of the meadow. The happy Milo walked by her side. Otis gloomily trailed behind.

They walked many miles through woods and fields, enjoying the bright reds and yellows of the late-autumn leaves.

Several weeks went by. Otis was feeling very bad. Milo always walked with Joyce and paid no attention to him. So Otis made a decision. "We're more than halfway home," he told Milo. "I'm going the rest of the way by myself."

"No, Otis," said Joyce. "We want you to stay with us."

But Otis turned and trotted away.

"Hey, Otis, where are you going?" Milo called.

But Otis didn't answer.

Milo and Joyce watched him until he disappeared over a hill. He never even looked back.

Otis had been on his own for just a few days when the first snowstorm of winter fell. The snow was cold and deep, and the snowdrifts were way over the little dog's head. He tried to make his way over the slippery hills of snow, but it wasn't easy.

Late one sunny afternoon as melting snow fell from the trees, Otis heard a dog crying out for help. "Over here. Over here," the dog pleaded.

She was trapped in a snowbank. Otis dug with his paws and struggled to pull her out. Finally he freed her.

She was beautiful. In fact, she looked just like him!

"I'm Sondra," she said. "Who are you?"

"Otis. I've never met a dog like you, Sondra." And for the first time in his rather serious life, Otis began acting very silly. He teased Sondra and nipped at her ears and chased her merrily through the snow.

Sondra had been spending the winter in a small but comfortable cave. She and Otis decided to stay there until spring. And even though the cold wind blew outside the cave, on the inside winter seemed very warm and cozy.

Meanwhile, Milo and Joyce had found a safe winter home inside a fallen tree trunk.

Late in the winter, Joyce was preparing to have kittens. "Are you okay, Joyce?" Milo asked. "Want some more dinner? Remember, you're eating for eight now."

"Milo," said Joyce excitedly, "I think it's time." Sure enough, Joyce began giving birth to one kitten after another.

Milo looked on in joy and amazement. "It's a girl!" he cried "And a boy! And another girl!"

"Four girls and three boys," Joyce counted. She smiled at Milo. "Congratulations, Dad!"

That same day, not too far away, Otis was in his cave with Sondra, who was about to give birth, too.

"Is it going to be soon?" Otis asked eagerly.

"Yes," Sondra replied.

A few minutes later, seeing his newborn puppy, Otis ran joyfully out into the snow, crying, "It's a boy! It's a boy!"

Sondra called him back inside. "Otis . . . you ran out a little too soon."

Immediately Otis saw what Sondra meant. He ran back outside, this time jumping and rolling in the snow and shouting, "It's a litter! It's a litter!"

Otis was very happy. But as the cold winter dragged on, he and Sondra faced a serious problem. There was too much winter left and too little food. Otis knew he had to go out and find something for all of them to eat. He said good-bye to Sondra and the puppies, left their cozy cave, and headed out into the deep snow.

Otis remembered a pond nearby. One day he had seen a bear scoop up some fish through a hole in the ice. "Maybe I'll be lucky and find some fish there," he told himself as he trudged over the snow.

But the bitter cold weather had frozen over the fishing hole. And the ice was too thick for Otis to break.

"No food here," he told himself sadly. Suddenly an icy wind brought a winter storm over the frozen pond. The wind was stinging his face like needles and his paws were numb from the cold. Wet snow clung to his face and covered his fur. He couldn't see where he was going. All he could see was a blizzard of white.

Otis was lost. Would he ever find his way back to the cave?

Otis tried to get to some shelter. But the snow was coming down too fast and the wind was blowing too hard. Finally the storm died down.

Otis shook the snow off his fur as best he could. He looked around. He had no idea where he was.

Then, far in the distance, he saw a small wooden farmhouse. He ran to the house and barked loudly to announce that there was a hungry dog outside.

Was anyone home?

Suddenly Otis heard a familiar voice. "My, my! Look what the snow blew in!"

Otis looked up at the top window to see Milo grinning down at him.

"You look hungry," Milo called. "How about some fish?"

"Okay," Otis said happily. "But not for me. For my puppies."

Milo was very surprised. "You have puppies? Me too!"

"You have *what*?" Otis cried.

"I mean kittens!" Milo said, laughing.

The farmer had several large racks of fish hanging outside the farmhouse. Milo pulled on a rope until one of the racks fell down to Otis. Otis took the rope and began to pull the fish back to his family.

"Hey, Otis," Milo called down to him. "I've really missed you."

"I've missed you, too," Otis confessed.

"When spring comes," Milo said, "why don't we meet, your family and mine. We can all travel back to the farm together."

"A wonderful idea," Otis agreed. Then he thanked Milo and hurried off across the snow, pulling the heavy load of fish to Sondra and the waiting puppies.

Spring arrived. Birds flew happily over the meadows. Bright flowers bloomed. Animals woke up and came out to enjoy the sunshine after their long winter naps.

Milo and Joyce brought their kittens out of the farmhouse. They waited on a high tree branch where they could watch for Otis.

Otis was having a little trouble getting his puppies organized. They were so excited by the beautiful warm weather, they just wanted to romp and play.

Finally Otis and Sondra arrived at the farmhouse. The two families saw each other for the first time.

Soon the puppies and kittens were playing and wrestling together in the warm spring grass.

Milo and Otis looked on proudly. They let their families get acquainted for a while. Then they gathered them together. They had a long journey ahead.

And what a glorious day for such a happy journey! Big dogs, little puppies, grown-up cats and kittens, all marched down the road together. And before long, Milo and Otis were finally back at the farm where their lives had begun.

When they left they were barely more than a kitten and a puppy themselves. And now, here they were coming back with little ones of their own, who would all grow up together. Very soon, the farm was in an uproar. The quacking, clucking and braying could be heard for miles as the news quickly spread — Milo and Otis were finally back home.